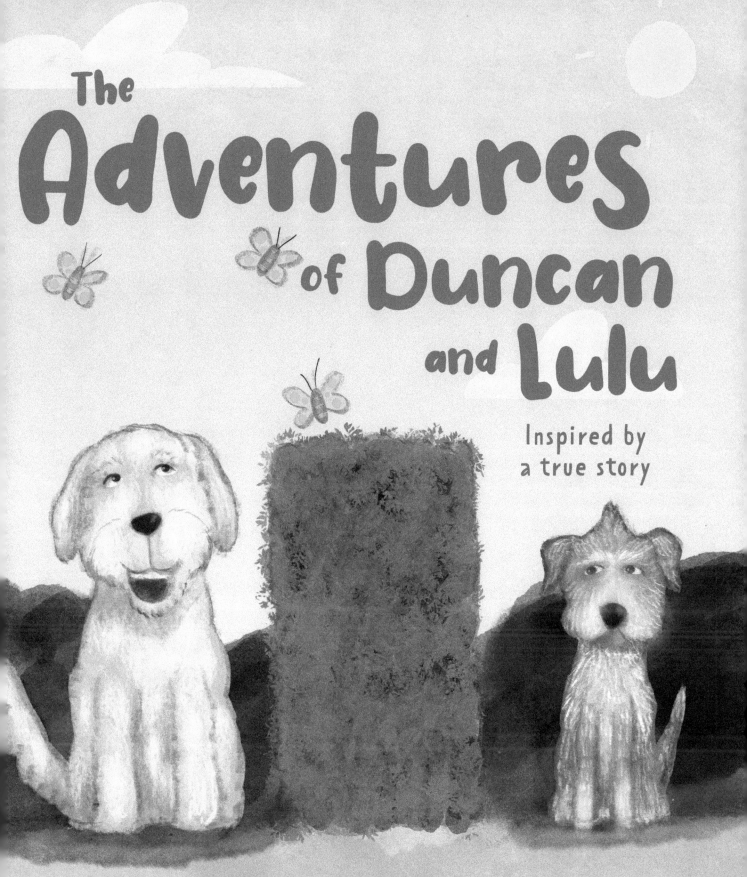

The Adventures of Duncan and Lulu

of Duncan and Lulu

Inspired by
a true story

Written by **Amanda Young** and **Traci Meyer**

Illustrated by **JP Roberts**

◆ FriesenPress

Suite 300 - 990 Fort St
Victoria, BC, V8V 3K2
Canada

www.friesenpress.com

ISBN
978-1-5255-8511-1 (Hardcover)
978-1-5255-8512-8 (Paperback)
978-1-5255-8513-5 (eBook)

1. JUVENILE FICTION, READERS, BEGINNER

Distributed to the trade by The Ingram Book Company

Amanda dedicates this book to her daughter.
Charlie, you inspire me with your fearless sense of
adventure, love of nature and passion for all animals.
You're a one of a kind human and I love you with
all my heart.

Traci dedicates this book to her loving family and
supportive boys. Zachary, your kinwdness is
everything. Jonah, your compassion is like nothing
else. Nathan, your thoughtfulness is endless.

It is just like any other sunny day in Cookie Court.

Duncan, a Goldendoodle with a heart of gold is outside sniffing dirt and chasing butterflies in his front yard. Suddenly, Duncan stops when he hears a car pull up at the house next door.

He immediately pokes his fuzzy face through the hedge between the two houses. The car door opens and Lulu, a scruffy dog with a line of fur in the shape of a mohawk, makes her way out of the car one paw at a time. The minute Duncan sees Lulu, his heart jumps for joy.

"Hey, moving in? What's with the mohawk? Is that how you wear your hair?" Duncan asks. Lulu ignores him.

Duncan is mesmerized by Lulu's big brown eyes. He watches as she courageously makes her way to her new home. Duncan shimmies his way out of the hedges. Twigs, leaves and cobwebs all over his body. He yells over the hedge, "Alrighty then, it was great to meet you! I'm Duncan, by the way! My friends call me **'THE FUNKINATOR.'**"

Duncan sits at his sewing machine with a picture of Lulu in his mind. Different colored fabric and stuffing are all over the floor. He eagerly makes a toy for his new neighbor.

The next morning, a very excited Duncan knocks on Lulu's front door. Lulu opens the door, and sees Duncan standing before her. He is grinning from ear to ear, the toy hedgehog is in his mouth.

Lulu turns her head from side to side. She says, "What do you want?"

Duncan turns *his* head from side to side. Confused, he drops the hedgehog and says, "To be your friend?" Lulu looks at him and says, "Please go away" and shuts the door. Surprised by this, Duncan says, "I see it's not a good time! I'll come back later!"

Duncan prances home knowing exactly what he needs to do. Surely, no one has ever baked cookies for her, and *not just any cookies*, his family's milk bone cookies.

With a pep in his step, he leaps into his kitchen, throws on his apron and chef hat, then flings the pantry door open. Clouds of flour fill the air as he rolls out the dough. He cuts out the cookies and throws them in the oven.

A few hours later Lulu is curled up tight in her bed, hedgehog in her arms. Lulu is sound asleep, when suddenly she wakes up to a delicious aroma that wafts through her bedroom window. Her nose begins frantically sniffing the air, she's licking her lips.

"What is that?" she says out loud. "Where's it coming from?" Suddenly, milk bones begin to fly at the window. Lulu slowly opens it, and a milk bone hits her directly in the face. Shocked, she slams the window shut.

Later that night, Lulu stands outside in the garden looking up at the moon. She hears a **HOOT, HOOT, HOOT.**

She takes a deep breath and bravely asks, "Who's there?"

A wise old owl appears in the tree above her. "Hello, my name is Mr. Owl. I am the eyes and ears of all the animals in Cookie Court neighborhood. I appear when someone needs help."

A tear rolls down Lulu's cheek.

The owl continues, "I see that you're struggling in your new home, I understand life has not been kind to you in the past. Lulu, you have a big heart and deserve to be happy. Duncan is trying to make friends with you. Is there a way to make space in your heart for him?"

Lulu says, "I've never had a friend before. I don't know how to trust anyone. And he's goofy and happy and nothing like me. We're too different."

The owl says, "It's okay to have friends that are different. You can learn new things from each other and it's important to take a chance with new people in life."

Lulu's head tilts as she ponders this.

"I'll be seeing you, Lulu. Remember, it's okay to open your heart. I'm looking out for you!" Mr. Owl **HOOTS** and flies away as fireflies float down from the starry sky and wink at Lulu.

Lulu stands in her backyard and looks over at Duncan's fence... It's been a whole week since she slammed the window on him and she hasn't seen him since. She wonders if Duncan has given up on her and says out loud, "I guess he's kind of funny... he did bake me cookies... should I give him a chance?"

The next morning Lulu stands at the window. She takes a big, brave, deep breath. She says to herself, "You can do this," and remembers what Mr. Owl said, "Take a chance." With that she opens the window and begins to throw milk bones at Duncan's window.

Duncan's face appears at the window. Lulu, with the hedgehog in her mouth, asks, "Want to play?"

Duncan, overjoyed, says, "I thought you'd never ask." He winks at her with his long eyelashes and says, "I'll meet you in the backyard."

The two dogs become fast friends and start exploring the city together. They pick up new friends along the way. Lulu looks at Duncan and says, "Let the adventures begin."

The real Duncan and Lulu

About the Authors

Traci, a busy mother to three boys, was convinced by her oldest that he "needed" a dog. Little did she know, Duncan the Goldendoodle would steal her heart and make her realize that she needed him, too. He changed their lives the minute he walked through the door and became Traci's fourth child in the center of their Hanukkah picture.

Amanda is a native Australian and mother to a fabulous, free-spirited daughter. She and her family love animals and have always had a dog. When an abused rescue named Lulu came into their lives, Amanda realized how much she would need to reorganize her life to help heal Lulu's heart and earn her trust. With much patience and time, and the help of the playful Goldendoodle next door who wouldn't give up—Lulu began trusting her new environment.

The love shared between these dogs is so special that Traci and Amanda wanted to share this journey of acceptance, trust and second chances. Little did they know how much fun *they* would have on the doggie playdates. The two have shared many laughs and have become great friends. They have even considered putting a doggie door between the two back yards. Traci and Amanda intend on donating a portion of each sale to the Last Call K9 Rescue.

Peanut butter milk bone cookie recipe

1 cup whole wheat flour

½ cup smooth peanut butter

¼ cup unsweetened apple sauce

¼ cup chicken stock

Preheat oven to 350 ˚F

Combine flour, peanut butter and apple sauce in a large mixing bowl. Add the stock and stir until combined.

Use your hands to make the dough into a ball.

Place dough onto a floured surface and roll out to about ¼ inch thick.

Using a medium bone-shaped cookie cutter, cut out cookies and place them on an ungreased baking sheet.

Bake for 20 minutes or until golden brown.

Healthy treats your dog will love. Enjoy!

CPSIA information can be obtained
at www.ICGtesting.com
Printed in the USA
LVHW070923091021
700000LV00006B/352